# Skating

## Pink Skate Party

## School

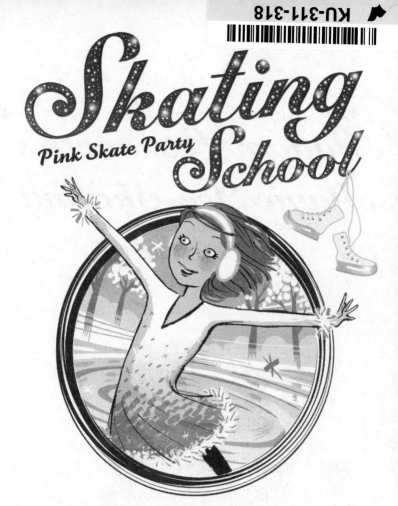

# Linda Chapman

Illustrated by Nellie Ryan

**PUFFIN**

# Madam Letsworth's Magic Ice-Skating Academy

FROST FAIRIES

MOLLY · HANNAH · EMILY · TILDA · ALICE

ICE OWLS

AMANDA  ZOE  HEATHER  TASHA  OLIVIA

SNOW FOXES

CAMILLA  TESS  CLARE  HELENA

*To Georgia Purcell – if you were ever at the Magic Ice-skating
Academy, you would be the Ice Princess*

PUFFIN BOOKS

Published by the Penguin Group
Penguin Books Ltd, 80 Strand, London WC2R ORL, England
Penguin Group (USA) Inc., 375 Hudson Street, New York, New York 10014, USA
Penguin Group (Canada), 90 Eglinton Avenue East, Suite 700, Toronto, Ontario, Canada M4P 2Y3
(a division of Pearson Penguin Canada Inc.)
Penguin Ireland, 25 St Stephen's Green, Dublin 2, Ireland (a division of Penguin Books Ltd)
Penguin Group (Australia), 250 Camberwell Road, Camberwell, Victoria 3124, Australia
(a division of Pearson Australia Group Pty Ltd)
Penguin Books India Pvt Ltd, 11 Community Centre, Panchsheel Park, New Delhi – 110 017, India
Penguin Group (NZ), 67 Apollo Drive, Rosedale, North Shore 0632, New Zealand
(a division of Pearson New Zealand Ltd)
Penguin Books (South Africa) (Pty) Ltd, 24 Sturdee Avenue, Rosebank, Johannesburg 2196, South Africa

Penguin Books Ltd, Registered Offices: 80 Strand, London WC2R ORL, England

puffinbooks.com

First published 2010
1

Text copyright © Linda Chapman, 2010
Illustrations copyright © Nellie Ryan, 2010
All rights reserved

The moral right of the author and illustrator has been asserted

Set in 15/22 pt Bembo
Typeset by Palimpsest Book Production Limited, Grangemouth, Stirlingshire
Made and printed in England by Clays Ltd, St Ives plc

British Library Cataloguing in Publication Data
A CIP catalogue record for this book is available from the British Library

ISBN: 978-0-141-32636-8

www.greenpenguin.co.uk

Mixed Sources
Product group from well-managed
forests and other controlled sources
www.fsc.org Cert no. SA-COC-1592
© 1996 Forest Stewardship Council

FSC

Penguin Books is committed to a sustainable future
for our business, our readers and our planet.
The book in your hands is made from paper
certified by the Forest Stewardship Council.

# Contents

# In the Magic Land of
# Ice and Winter . . .

Everything looked just as it always did. A
blanket of crisp snow covered the fields
and meadows, towns and villages. Frozen
lakes glittered in the rays of the pale sun
and a mist hung over the tops of the
jagged mountains. Silvery robins darted
from tree to tree while white fluffy fox
cubs tumbled after each other. But the

ice sylphs who lived in the land knew
something was different.

At the edge of the land, one of the
mountains had changed shape.
Something had curled around it, great
wings folded flat. Its dark-red scaly sides
moved in and out, and every so often it
would open its mouth and a great jet of
fire would stream out.

The headteacher of the Magic Ice-
skating Academy, Madame Letsworth, sat
at her desk looking down a list of girls'
names. Beside some of them were ticks,

others had question marks and a few had crosses.

Madame Letsworth rubbed her forehead. The ice sylphs' wonderful land was melting and they *had* to get the dragon to move. One of the human girls at the school could help them by becoming the Ice Princess.

'But if we don't choose the right girl then the magic won't work,' Madame Letsworth murmured. Her eyes flicked

from one name to another: Hannah
Peters, Emily Walker, Molly Wang,
Amanda Duval, Zoe Hassan, Alice
Jenson . . . Which of the girls really had
the qualities they needed?

Hopefully the competition that week
would help her decide.

## Chapter One
### *Practice Makes Perfect*

Molly leapt into the air, turning as she jumped, her straight black hair flying around her face. She landed on one leg, but, as she did so, she wobbled and collapsed in a heap on the floor of the ballet studio.

Emily giggled. 'You'd better not do that in the competition!' Together with their other friend, Hannah, she hauled Molly to her feet.

'It's much easier on skates,' Molly sighed.

'It's good to walk through a new routine off the ice though,' Hannah sensibly reminded her. 'It helps to learn it and that's really important right now.

We've only got six days before the competition.'

A shiver of excitement ran down Emily's spine. The evening before, the girls at the Magic Ice-skating Academy had found out that their next competition was to skate a two-minute routine. Certain moves had to be included – an upright spin, a double jump combination, a drag and a spiral, but it was up to the girls to choreograph the routines for themselves. They also had to choose their own music and design their own costumes.

'We want to see how well you can put a routine together,' Madame Letsworth had told them. 'Each judge will award two marks, one for technical ability and one for artistic interpretation. The winner of this week's competition will receive a pair of pink skates with silver laces.'

Molly took off her shoes and began to move around the studio again, sliding in her socks as if she had skates on.

'I'll do a double flip, double toe loop here and then my drag, then speed up and do a double axel followed by a layback spin to finish.' She ended in the middle of the room, her arms above her head. 'There – done!' she declared. 'Your turn, Em.'

Emily tucked her shoulder-length brown hair behind her ears. 'I think I'll put my music on to help me picture my routine. I always remember better with music.'

She went over to the purple music box in the corner. It was covered with silver buttons divided into columns with different titles like 'lively', 'slow', 'sad'. But rather than pressing any of these, Emily lifted the lid.

Inside were lots of wheels and gears and levers as well as three silvery-blue dragons, each the size of Emily's hand. They chirruped when they saw her.

'Hi,' Emily said. 'Would you mind playing some music for me? It was number fifty-two.'

'*Of course,*' one of the dragons squeaked cheerfully in dragon language.

Emily closed the lid. She loved the fact that at the Magic Ice-skating Academy there were creatures like dragons. It was going to be really strange when she went back to her old life and used a normal CD player again!

*Everything's going to be strange when we go back home*, she realized.

Although she missed her family and friends, Emily loved being at skating school. It had been like a dream come true when she had been whisked away by magic to the Land of Ice and Winter three weeks ago. When she had found she could stay at the Ice-skating Academy there, taking lessons to improve her ice-skating with the other human girls who had been chosen, and that no time would pass in the human world while she was away, she had immediately said yes. She definitely wanted to stay!

At the end of six weeks, one of the fourteen girls was going to be chosen to be the Ice Princess. Madame Letsworth had told them that this girl would have

to perform a task to help the ice sylphs
who lived in the land. If the Ice Princess
performed it successfully, she would be
granted a wish.

Emily longed to be the person chosen
to be Ice Princess. However, there were
still three weeks until the teachers made
their decision and, while she was at this
magical school, Emily was determined to
make the most of every moment.

She walked to the centre of the room.
She had chosen a piece of lively, soaring
music for her routine, which reminded

her of birds swooping through the air. As she took her starting position, the music began to play.

Emily set off round the studio. 'First I'll do some crossovers and then turn, skate backwards and into the double jump we have to do. After that, I'll go into the drag.' She crouched down, one leg behind her, arms and head thrown back. On the ice, she would be gliding gracefully of course.

'Cool!' called Molly approvingly. 'That'll look good, Em!'

Emily continued, finishing with an upright spin. She could only turn round once on the floor, but hopefully on the ice she would be able to spin round lots of times.

'It's a lovely routine, Emily,' said

Hannah. 'It really suits you.'

'I can't wait to be doing it on the ice,' said Emily. She did a lot of ballet back in the human world, but, although dancing was fun, it was nowhere near as good as skating. She loved the feeling of speed and the sensation of flying she had when she was on the ice. When she was skating really well, Emily felt as if every bit of her was sparkling.

'We'll go to the rink straight after our ballet lesson,' said Molly, turning a double cartwheel.

Emily grinned. 'Imagine if you could do that on the ice.'

'Don't tempt her!' Hannah said quickly. Molly was very daring.

Molly's brown eyes twinkled. 'Maybe I could try . . .'

'No!' Hannah and Emily both chorused.

'Ohhhh.' Molly pretended to look disappointed. 'You two are *so* boring.'

The bell rang to signal the end of lunch. 'We'd better get ready for ballet,' said Hannah.

They hurried through to the changing room where all the other girls were gathering. As they changed out of the skating dresses they wore most of the time into pale-blue leotards and ballet shoes, Emily realized something. 'If I was at home, it would be my birthday on Sunday,' she said.

'Really? Then we should have a party!' said Molly.

'But it's not Emily's proper birthday,' Hannah pointed out. 'When we go home, she'll still be the same age as when she left. All of us will be, because no time will have passed.'

'And Sunday's the day of the competition anyway,' said Emily. 'There'll be too much else going on −' She broke off as the other girls came into the changing room followed by Madame Breshnev, the small, neat ballet teacher.

'Into the studio when you're ready,

please, girls!' she called.

Hannah, Molly and Emily followed
their teacher back into the ballet studio
and started bending and stretching at the
barre. Emily bent her knees in a deep
plié, but in her head she was jumping
and spinning above the ice rink.
Birthdays were fun to think about, but
not as much fun as ice-skating!

# Chapter Two
## *At the Ice Rink*

*Push and glide, push and glide . . .*

Emily skated backwards. Kicking the
toe of her left boot into the ice, she
pushed up with her right leg. The next
moment, she was spinning round
weightlessly in the air, her arms tight to
her sides. She landed neatly on one foot
and glided on. Happiness rushed through
her. It had taken her a while to learn

how to do a double toe loop, but she could do it really well now and was going to perform it in her routine. She practised the move again, determined to perfect it.

The rink was one of Emily's favourite places in the school. The roof was made of glass and the ice was regularly smoothed by the frost fairies, tiny creatures about two centimetres high. As well as smoothing the ice, they did all the cooking and cleaning. A cloud of them clustered near the changing room, talking to each other in their high-pitched voices, their silver wings a blur.

A few of them saw Emily looking over and waved. She waved back.

All around her, everyone else was practising hard. Tilda and Alice, who shared the Frost Fairies dorm with Emily, Molly and Hannah, were working together on sit spins, and Amanda, another of Emily's friends, was doing a beautiful spiral, her arms thrown back dramatically. Molly was over on the far side of the rink practising a spin, turning quickly on the spot with her body arched back. She could spin faster than anyone else at the school.

Emily looked round for Hannah. Whereas Molly was small and full of energy, always spinning faster and jumping higher than anyone else, Hannah was tall and slim and looked very graceful on the ice. She was practising a difficult combination of jumps. She wasn't managing to get it right, but she kept trying.

Emily decided to do another double toe loop. She knew she had to practise each move over and over again. When they had started at the school, she had been the least experienced skater there. She had practised hard and really improved, but she still couldn't do all the really difficult jumps and spins that some of the others could. However, Emily hoped that if she skated each of the moves she knew as perfectly as possible, she might still have a chance in the competition.

She glided backwards and built up speed again . . . But as she landed this time, she caught an edge on the ice and fell over.

'What a surprise! Emily hits the ice once again!' drawled a voice behind her.

Emily didn't have to look round to know
who was speaking. There was only one
girl at the Academy who was mean if
someone fell over – Camilla Meredith.

Unhurt, Emily scrambled to her feet.
Camilla skated round in front of her. She
had glossy strawberry-blonde hair,
creamy skin and big green eyes. But

although she was beautiful on the outside, Emily had soon found out that she wasn't so nice on the inside.

'You should be doing a clown routine then it won't matter if you fall over all the time!' Camilla laughed scornfully and skated back to where her friends were standing.

Emily ignored her. Camilla had been her friend in the first week, but they had fallen out when Emily had also wanted to be friends with Hannah and Molly. Ever since then, Camilla had been really mean to her. Trying to push Camilla's comments out of her mind, Emily had another go at the double jump and this time landed it accurately. Triumph flooded through her. She glanced to see if Camilla had been watching, but

Camilla was too busy showing off in the centre of the rink.

As Emily slowed down to get her breath back, she heard Camilla's voice floating across the ice as all her friends congratulated her on the jump she had just done. 'Oh, that's nothing.' Camilla's eyes flicked to where Hannah was still doggedly practising. 'For my routine, I'm going to do a double lutz–double toe loop.'

'That would be really cool!' said Tess, Camilla's best friend.

'Will you be able to do it?' asked Helena, one of the other girls from the Snow Foxes dorm.

'Course I will,' said Camilla confidently. 'Watch!'

She skated off. Emily glanced towards

Hannah. Emily was sure Camilla had decided to do the double lutz–double toe loop combination because that was exactly what Hannah was practising and getting wrong. Camilla would love to prove she could do it better. Luckily Hannah was so busy focusing on her own skating that she wasn't taking any notice of Camilla.

Camilla skated backwards faster and faster and then pushed down with her right foot and spun round into the air. When she landed, she took off again straight away, spinning round tightly two more times before landing neatly and skating on, her arms gracefully outstretched as if inviting applause.

Her friends all clapped obediently.

'See!' Camilla skated back to them

with a triumphant smile on her face.

'You're *so* going to win this week if you get all your jumps right,' said Tess enviously.

'I hope so.' Camilla glanced towards Hannah, who had just pulled out of the second part of the same combination.

'Camilla is *so* annoying!' a voice burst out behind Emily. Emily turned round and saw Molly skating up to her.

She nodded in agreement. 'I hope she doesn't win the competition.'

'Me too,' said Molly. A thoughtful look crossed her face. 'Maybe if I could do a triple jump it would really impress the judges.'

'A triple jump,' echoed Emily. That meant turning round three times in the air after jumping off the ice. 'Could you do that?'

'Well, I've never landed one before, but there's a first time for everything,' Molly said cheerfully. 'I'll try one.'

She skated away across the rink and threw herself into the air. Emily saw her go round once, twice, but as she was going round the third time, she lost momentum and had to pull out, almost falling on her nose.

'Full marks for style, Molly!' yelled Camilla. 'If you're in the skating-like-an-

ostrich competition, that is!' Her friends all giggled.

Hannah skated over. 'What were you trying to do?'

'A triple toe loop,' admitted Molly.

'But that's much too . . .' Hannah stopped. Emily was sure she had been about to say 'hard', but Hannah seemed to think better of it and tactfully changed her words. 'Are you quite sure you're ready for that, Molly? I know you're a brilliant skater, but don't you think you should wait a bit?'

'Why wait?' Molly said airily. 'If I get it right, just think how awesome it'll be!'

A whistle blew and the three skating teachers arrived: Madame Letsworth, who taught the advanced skaters –

Hannah, Molly, Camilla, Zoe and
Amanda; Madame Li, who taught the
intermediate skaters; and Monsieur
Carvallio, who taught the beginner
skaters – the group that Emily was in.

The teachers skated on to the ice and
the students gathered round them.
Madame Letsworth blew her whistle
again and the lesson began.

Emily loved her skating lessons.
Monsieur Carvallio was a dark-skinned
ice sylph with kind eyes. He was quick
to pick up on her faults, but always gave
her plenty of praise and, though she
would never say it out loud because she
hated boasting, she could see that in the
three weeks she had been at the school
she had improved a lot more than Tilda

and Heather, the other two in the
beginners' group.

Monsieur Carvallio wanted them to
work on spirals today. They were one of
Emily's favourite moves. As she glided
round with one leg in the air, she felt
balanced and elegant, just like a bird in
flight.

'Excellent,' Monsieur Carvallio praised.
'That was beautiful, Emily.' She smiled.
After Camilla's mean words earlier, it was
lovely to be praised. She glanced over at
the advanced group to see what they
were doing.

They were practising their double
axels, a particularly hard jump. The
elation Emily had felt at Monsieur
Carvallio's words faded slightly. Although
she had improved loads, she knew she

was still nowhere near as good as the skaters in the advanced group.

*That's OK*, she told herself, trying to be positive. *You can't expect to be as good as them, but that doesn't mean you should stop trying. If you get your routine as near perfect as possible, you might still do well in the competition.*

Determination filled her. She was going to practise and practise and do everything she could to improve! She really wanted to win those pink skates!

## Chapter Three
### Costume Designing

After they had finished skating, the girls had some free time before supper. They went to the common room to design their costumes. The frost fairies were going to be making them and the girls had been told to give their designs in as soon as possible. Emily fetched some paper and pens and she, Hannah and Molly sat down on one of the sofas.

Emily didn't have to think for long. She loved drawing and could already see the costume in her head. She drew sheet after sheet until she was happy. Molly was working almost as quickly while Hannah sighed and chewed her pencil.

'I've got the perfect idea,' Amanda announced smugly, sitting back in her chair. 'My music is like flamenco music so I'm going to have a flamenco dancer's costume in red and black, only with a short skirt. I'll look really cool!'

Emily saw a few of the others roll their eyes and smiled to herself. Amanda never changed. She could be really boastful at times, but over the last few weeks she had proved that she could be nice too.

'Done!' Molly declared, holding out a piece of paper. She had drawn a red

skating dress with an orange, red and
yellow skirt.

'That's great,' said Hannah admiringly.
Molly's routine was a piece of music
from an opera where people were
dancing round a fire.

'You should add some sequins in here,'
Emily said, pointing to the neckline.

'And make the sleeves longer – it'll show off the line of your arms better.'

'Great! Thanks, Em,' said Molly, quickly adding to her drawing. 'Have you done yours?'

Emily nodded. She had decided to go for a pale-blue dress with deep-turquoise stripes. It was sleeveless with a short floaty skirt.

'That's beautiful,' said Molly.

'I wish mine was as good,' Hannah sighed. 'Look.' She held out her drawing of a pale-green dress.

It was hard to know what to say. The dress was just plain green with nothing on it. It looked very dull. 'Oh, that's um . . . a nice colour,' Emily managed to say.

Hannah ran a hand through her

blonde hair. 'I'm no good at thinking up dresses. My mum does all that for me back at home. I just get on with the skating.'

'Maybe Emily could do a design for you,' Molly suggested.

'Yes, or we could just add to this one,' said Emily. 'I could help you.'

Hannah looked embarrassed. 'No, don't worry. After all, the competition's about our skating ability really. It'll be fine –'

She broke off as the common-room door opened and Camilla came in with Tess and Helena. 'Did you see that frost fairy's face when I gave her my design,' she was saying. 'I thought her eyes were going to pop out of her silly head!'

'I wish I'd thought of wearing a catsuit,' said Tess.

'A catsuit!' Molly echoed from the sofa.

Camilla looked smug. 'Yeah. It's silver and black. It'll look amazing.'

'Amazingly weird,' Molly said.

Camilla gave her a withering look. 'If I wanted your opinion, I'd have asked for it, Molly.'

'And if I wanted to look stupid on the ice, I'd wear a catsuit!' Molly grinned.

Camilla turned sharply on her heel and marched to the far end of the room.

For the rest of that evening all they talked about were their routines.

*Just six days to go*, thought Emily as she got into bed. *Who is going to win?* Shutting her eyes, she started to go through all the different moves in her head. Lost in happy thoughts of spirals and double toe loops, she fell fast asleep.

When Emily woke up the next morning, she saw Tilda and Alice getting dressed in their outdoor clothes – trousers and padded jackets.

'Where are you going?' she asked, sitting up in bed.

'Out to see the huskies,' said Alice. In the gardens there were kennels where the school huskies were kept. They were used for pulling sledges to get around the land.

'I might have known,' Emily said with a grin. Alice was animal-mad and Tilda, being her best friend, went everywhere with her – which usually meant down to the kennels.

'Trakin, the head husky handler, has said he'll start teaching us how to drive husky sledges if we go early today,' said Tilda. 'You should come, Emily.'

Emily loved the huskies, and the thought of learning to drive a husky sledge was very tempting, but what about the competition? She wanted to go to the rink and practise before breakfast. 'No, I'm going to go skating.' She frowned. 'Shouldn't you be practising too?'

Alice shrugged. 'I'm not going to win so what's the point?'

'You might,' said Emily in surprise.

'I won't,' said Alice. 'Anyway, I'd rather see the huskies.'

'OK then. Well, have fun,' said Emily, getting up and pulling an ice-skating dress out of the neat little wardrobe at the end of her bed. The girls each had a selection of practice dresses and Emily chose a soft one in white and pale pink with a scooped neckline and long sleeves. She laid the dress on her bed along with her cream tights.

Alice and Tilda had said goodbye and left. Molly and Hannah were still asleep. Emily grinned and went round to the table between their beds, where there was a glass of water. She dipped her finger in and dropped water on to their faces. They both woke up with a start.

'Emily!' groaned Molly, throwing a
pillow at her.

'Come on, lazybones!' Emily said,
pulling their duvets off. 'We've got some
practising to do!'

## Chapter Four
## *Found in the Woods*

Emily glided round the rink on one leg, her head down near her knees, her arms flung back as if they were wings. She felt she really was soaring through the air – just like a bird. Lowering her leg, she started skating backwards, faster and faster, until she launched herself into a double flip. But she landed badly on two feet instead of one and tutted at herself.

It wasn't good enough. She was going to have to do better than that if she wanted to win.

Frowning in concentration, Emily tried again and again.

Hannah came over. 'Em, I was thinking about my dress when I went to bed last night. My design is OK, isn't it?'

'Yeah.' Emily was distracted by the jump not working. *I need more height*, she thought anxiously.

'Do you think I should just scrap that design and do something else?'

Emily hesitated, torn between wanting to help and wanting to get her double flip right. 'It's fine,' she said, her feet itching to start skating again.

'Oh,' Hannah said. 'OK.'

Emily skated off. For a moment she felt

bad she hadn't talked more about Hannah's costume, but she pushed the thought away. *Concentrate on what you're doing*, she told herself. *You know you have to focus if you want to win. You need to skate faster . . .*

She launched into her flip, but her body felt wrong and she stumbled on landing.

'Good jump, Emily,' Camilla said sarcastically as she glided past.

Emily's practice didn't go well that

morning. Her jumps just wouldn't come right and her spins seemed off-centre. *I'm going to have to get better than this*, she realized as she came off the ice. *I'm never going to do well in the competition if I make dumb mistakes. I'm going to have to practise harder and harder.*

She was just putting her boots away, feeling cross with herself, when Alice and Tilda came hurrying into the changing area. There was a look of excitement about them.

'What's up with you two?' Molly called from where she was changing.

'You'll never guess what just happened!' Tilda said. 'We were out in the woods, practising husky driving, and we saw this little baby ice dragon on the ground, all on his own.'

44

'We picked him up and took him back to the kennels. Trakin said he must have dropped out of his mother's pouch when she was flying overhead. If we hadn't found him, he'd have died!' said Alice.

'Where is he now?' asked Emily.

'Trakin told Madame Longley and she's put him in the walk-in cupboard in her classroom in a big box. Come and see him!'

Emily, Hannah and Molly didn't need any more urging. They jumped to their feet and followed Alice and Tilda to the classroom where they had their lessons on the creatures and geography of the magic land.

Alice opened the cupboard and Emily caught her breath. Sitting inside a large cardboard box was a baby ice dragon! He was the size of a mouse and a very pale blue. As she watched, he snorted and ice crystals puffed out of his snout.

'He's gorgeous,' she said, sinking down beside the box.

'We've called him Charlie,' said Alice.

Emily chirruped to him. The dragon's eyes gleamed like dark jewels and he chirruped back.

'What does he eat?' Hannah asked.

'Mushed-up leaves,' said Alice.

'Of course,' said Emily, remembering a class they'd had once on ice dragons. 'The mothers usually chew the leaves up first, don't they?'

'Yes. We're not going to do that though!' Tilda grinned. 'We're just going to mush them up with a pestle and mortar.' She pointed to a round bowl with its grinding stick.

'He has to be fed every hour at the moment and he needs lots of company too,' said Alice. 'Madame Longley said that ice dragons don't like being on their own, but he's still too little to be put in with the other dragons.'

'So we're going to look after him until he's big enough,' said Tilda. 'Will you lot help?'

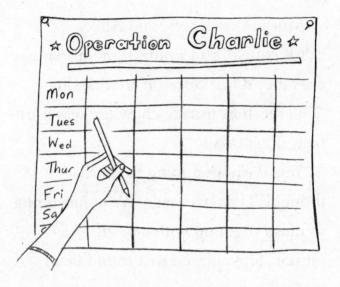

'Of course!' Emily said and Hannah and Molly nodded.

'I'll draw up a rota then,' said Alice.

Molly stroked the tiny dragon. 'It'll be Operation Charlie,' she said. He blinked his dark eyes and snorted ice crystals into her face.

## Chapter Five
## *Trying Too Hard*

The next few days passed very quickly.
Emily spent all her time out of classes
practising her routine. She hardly
thought about anything except for the
competition. She went to sleep thinking
about it and woke up thinking about it –
she even skated it over and over again in
her dreams! However, to her intense
frustration, she seemed to be doing her

routine less well now than when she had first thought it up.

It began to seem like the more she tried and the longer she practised, the worse she got. She spent so much time on the ice that she hardly did anything with her friends. The only thing that Emily did make sure she made time for was looking after the baby ice dragon.

'I wish I was better at my routine, Charlie,' Emily told the dragon as she took her turn to feed him at morning break on Thursday. He flapped his way out of the open box and landed on one of the shelves, where he proceeded to joyfully pull out all the papers from one of Madame Longley's folders.

'No, don't do that,' Emily said quickly. The little dragon had got very good at

getting the lid off his box and escaping.
Alice had made him some dragon toys
and got some pieces of bark for him to
chew on, but he always seemed to be up
to mischief – climbing the curtains or
chewing up important papers. Emily
scooped the baby dragon up and moved
him back into his box. He squawked in
annoyance.

'I'm sorry,' Emily told him as the
squawk changed to a plaintive squeak. 'I
know you don't like being left on your
own, but I really have to go now and
practise again. One of the others will be
here later.'

Shutting the door of the cupboard
behind her, she hurried quickly away.

When Emily got to the rink, Alice came
over. 'How was Charlie?'

'Fine,' replied Emily.

'I'm really worried about him getting
bored and being on his own,' said Alice.
'Madame Longley said I can introduce
him to the other dragons in a week or so,
but what are we going to do until then?
He's getting so naughty – and he's so
good at escaping.'

'Mmm,' Emily said, not really listening as she put on her skates. In her head she was already going through her routine.

'Will you help me try and think of something?' asked Alice.

'Yeah,' Emily mumbled. 'Maybe later.' She headed on to the ice and with a deep sigh started her routine.

She felt tense and uncomfortable inside. With every mistake she made that day, a feeling of panic started to build inside her. What would she do if she got things wrong in the competition? She watched the other girls, hoping to pick up some tips. Maybe she should copy them? Molly was so fast and Amanda so dramatic. Camilla was very elegant and Zoe so accurate . . .

'Em!' Emily looked round. Hannah

was skating over. 'Can I talk to you a minute? I'm worried about Molly.'

Emily nodded vaguely, but her thoughts were on her own bad performance. 'Do you think I should skate faster into my double flip?' she asked Hannah. 'Molly and Camilla always skate really fast.'

Hannah blinked. 'It might help,' she

said. 'But look, about Molly. She keeps falling over all the time when she's trying the triple jump and –'

'Hang on. Let me just try it.' Emily skated off. She wanted to see what would happen if she skated even faster into the double flip. She sped up, lifted into the air, spun round, tensed and . . .

*SLAM!*

She ended up on the ice. Giving an annoyed exclamation, she stood up.

'Are you OK?' Hannah called out.

'Fine!' Emily snapped. She saw Hannah's look of surprise and felt bad. 'Sorry, I'm just trying to get this right,' she sighed.

Deciding to try again, Emily began to skate backwards round the rink, but as she did so, she saw Molly skating into another triple toe loop. Molly's face was set and flushed.

*Maybe Hannah's right and we should stop her*, Emily realized. She hesitated and then started to skate over. 'Molly!'

But Molly wasn't listening. She dug her toe pick into the ice and propelled herself upwards, but she was going too fast. She spun round and lost control. Falling out of the spin, she landed on one leg. It seemed to buckle beneath her and she thudded heavily on to the ice. Crying out in pain, she clasped her leg with both hands.

'My ankle,' she gasped as Emily and Hannah both raced over.

Emily knelt down beside her. Tears sprung to Molly's eyes. 'It really hurts!'

'I'll get help!' said Hannah quickly.

Molly started to cry. Emily felt awful. She hugged her tightly. 'It'll be OK,' she said. 'Madame Letsworth will be here in a moment.'

It felt like they waited ages, but it was only really a few minutes before Hannah returned with Madame Letsworth and Monsieur Carvallio. By then, everyone else on the rink had noticed something was the matter and had skated over.

'Now, make some space, please, girls,' called Madame Letsworth.

Monsieur Carvallio examined Molly's foot and then scooped her up. 'We'd better get you to the sick bay.'

'But what's the matter with it? What have I done?' Molly said through her tears.

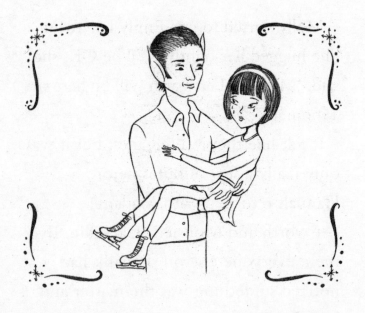

'We need to get the doctor to look at you,' Monsieur Carvallio said. 'Come on.'

Emily and Hannah exchanged worried glances and followed the teachers and Molly off the ice.

## Chapter Six
### *Four Days Off*

'No skating for at least four days!' Molly exclaimed in horror. 'But I'll miss the competition!'

The doctor, a short ice sylph with glasses and a beard, looked at her sympathetically. 'I'm sorry, but you have strained your ankle very badly and you must rest it. You were lucky not to have broken it. Absolutely no skating until Monday.'

Molly went very quiet. Emily felt awful for her. She knew how upset she would be if she had to miss the competition. She and Hannah had been allowed to come to the sick bay. Matron, the school nurse, was there with Madame Letsworth.

Madame Letsworth touched Molly's hand. 'It's only four days, Molly. You really don't want to do any more damage.'

Molly nodded, but Emily could see her chewing her lower lip and knew she was trying to hold back the tears.

'You'll be fine here, my dear,' said Matron kindly. 'I'll make sure you rest.' She had grey hair, neatly tied back in a bun, and a kind, no-nonsense manner. 'Now, let me get you a drink and maybe your

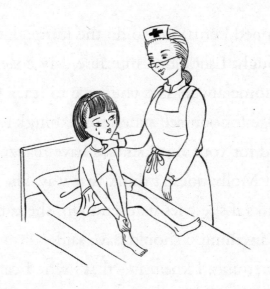

friends can go and get you some clothes, a toothbrush and some books.' She looked enquiringly at Emily and Hannah.

'Of course,' said Hannah. 'We'll get them right away.'

She and Emily set off to the dorm. 'Poor Molly!' Emily burst out as they hurried down the corridor.

'I know,' agreed Hannah. 'I wish I'd

stopped her trying to do the jump, but I thought I shouldn't interfere. My coach at home always says you have to learn to judge for yourself when something's too hard for you. But I should have realized that Molly doesn't think that way. She thinks if she tries hard enough, she can do anything. I should have said something. I knew it – that's why I came over to talk to you about it.'

Emily squeezed her hand. 'I should have listened.'

'It's OK. You were busy practising,' said Hannah.

*That's not a good enough excuse.* Emily felt awful. She hadn't been a very good friend.

As they went into the Frost Fairies dorm, they saw that every bed had a package wrapped in tissue paper at the end of it. 'What are they?' Emily said, picking hers up. It felt soft and through the tissue she saw a flash of blue. 'It's my costume!' she realized in delight.

She unwrapped the tissue paper. There was a beautiful turquoise-and-white velvet costume inside. It was perfect! The material was beautifully soft and there were two deep-turquoise bands at the front just as she had drawn it. But as Emily glanced at Molly's bed next to hers, her excitement faded. Molly's dress was there, but Molly wouldn't get to wear it now.

Hannah had taken her dress out. She held it up and looked at it with an expression of disappointment. It was a lovely sea-green, but very plain. 'It's a bit dull, isn't it?'

'It's plain, but that's OK,' said Emily tactfully. She couldn't help feeling a bit guilty as she remembered how Molly had suggested she help Hannah with her design. She should have insisted.

Hannah forced a smile. 'Yeah. It's fine.' Putting the dress down, she went to Molly's cupboard. 'Come on, let's collect Molly's things and get back to her.'

Hannah busied herself getting clothes

and a nightdress for Molly and Emily
went to fetch Molly's toothbrush and
flannel. 'What shall we do about her
dress?'

'Leave it here. She's upset enough as it
is,' said Hannah and they headed back to
the sick bay.

'Madame Letsworth has decided that
you can be excused this morning's
lessons,' said Matron. 'You can stay here
and keep Molly company. I think she
could do with some cheering up.' She
looked at Molly and her voice softened
slightly. 'Injuries happen to all skaters,
my dear. You will be back on the ice in
next to no time.' She left the room.

'She's right,' said Hannah, sitting down
on Molly's bed. 'You'll be better soon.'

'Not soon enough,' Molly said in a

small voice. A tear trickled down her cheek. 'I've got to miss the competition.'

'It's horrible, I know,' said Emily.

'No, you *don't* know!' burst out Molly. 'It's not just horrible! It's the worst thing that's ever happened to me!'

She started to cry in earnest. Hannah and Emily both hugged her, but Molly wouldn't be comforted. 'It's not fair!' she sobbed.

Eventually her tears subsided and she lay back down and turned on to her side, wincing with pain as she moved her leg. 'It's OK, you don't have to stay here. You can go.'

'I'm going to have to,' said Hannah, glancing at the clock on the wall. 'I'm supposed to be feeding Charlie.'

'I'll stay though,' said Emily.

'I'll come back later,' promised Hannah, getting up. She left and, for a long moment, there was silence in the room.

Molly broke it. 'You might as well go, Em,' she snapped. 'Go and practise or something. I know it's really important to you right now.'

'Molly, I'm not going anywhere,' Emily told her. 'You're hurt. As if I'd leave you on your own to go and practise!'

'Well, I'm not going to be any fun to be around,' said Molly.

'You don't have to be fun,' Emily told her softly. 'I just want to be here with you.'

Molly swallowed. 'Thanks, Em,' she said with a small smile.

★

At first, Emily and Molly just talked a bit and then Emily got out the books, but Molly didn't feel like reading so Emily looked around and found some board games in a wardrobe in the room. They played snakes-and-ladders and then ludo. After a while, Molly cheered up a bit. Matron brought them in a big plate of sandwiches for lunch and Hannah also returned.

'Everyone's really worried about you,' she said to Molly.

Molly managed a grin. 'Even Camilla?'

'Well, OK, maybe Camilla wasn't head of the queue of people asking about you,' Hannah admitted, her eyes twinkling. 'But everyone else wanted to know how you are. They're all making get-well cards, and Tilda and Alice were talking

about smuggling a husky pup in here to cheer you up.'

Molly's eyes lit up. 'Tell them they must! I'm going to go mad with boredom here when you two are in lessons. Oh, I can't believe I was so stupid. I should have just given up that jump – it was too hard. I'm not going to be that stupid ever again!'

Emily checked the clock. 'I'm on Charlie duty now,' she said. 'I'm supposed to be playing with him this lunchtime so he doesn't get too bored. I'll come back before lessons start this afternoon though.'

'And I'll stay while Emily's gone,' said Hannah.

Molly grinned. 'You'll be on Molly duty.'

'Yeah,' Hannah told her. 'Just don't start climbing up the curtains!'

Molly giggled, looking much more like her usual self. 'I won't do that, but if you're not careful, I might chew up some of Matron's papers!'

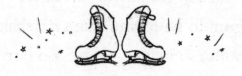

## Chapter Seven
### Helping Out

Emily found that there was quite a lot of tidying up to do in the cupboard. Charlie had tipped his water bowl into a pair of shoes that Madame Longley kept on a shelf and then he had shredded up a duster and a rubber. It was almost like walking into a snow storm. Emily cleared it all away and then played with him, tickling his tummy until he chirruped with glee and making him paper tubes to blow puffs of ice down. 'What are we going to do with you?' she said, shaking her head.

Charlie hopped over to Emily, rubbing his head against her and looking up at her with eager dark eyes. He nudged her pocket with his nose. She smiled. 'No, you're not coming round in my pocket!'

She picked him up and put him back

in his cardboard box, trying to ignore his squeaks of protest. Then she shut the lid as firmly as she could and headed back to Molly's room.

All through lessons that afternoon, Emily found herself feeling distracted. She couldn't stop thinking about how she hadn't been a very good friend recently. It wasn't just Molly, it was Hannah too. She had hardly said a word about her costume and Emily was sure Hannah was secretly upset about it.

*I should have made her let me help*, Emily thought. *I could have thought up something so much better. And then there's Alice. She wanted me to help her think up something to keep Charlie out of mischief and I didn't, and he's so bored and fed up . . .*

She stopped. Molly was bored and fed up and Charlie was bored and fed up. Maybe they could both be helped . . . Emily caught her breath. Yes, of course! She'd just had a brilliant idea! There was just one person she had to convince . . .

'Have an ice dragon here? In sick bay?' Matron stared at Emily.

'He's only a baby and he's all on his own. Molly could look after him,' Emily said.

'Oh, yes! Please, Matron,' Molly begged. 'I'd love it.'

'Oh, please, Matron,' added Hannah. Emily had told her about her plan straight after the lesson and they had both raced back to sick bay.

Matron looked at them all and her

74

expression softened. 'Oh, all right,' she said. 'But he'd better not get up to any mischief.'

'He's only naughty when he's on his own,' Emily assured her. Matron nodded and went out.

'Thanks so much, Em!' Molly exclaimed. 'It's a fantastic idea!'

Emily smiled. 'I'll go and tell Tilda and Alice.'

She hurried downstairs and checked in the common room. The frost fairies were in there fluttering around, tidying up. Tilda and Alice were there too. Emily quickly told them her idea.

'That's a great plan!' said Alice, looking relieved. 'It was going to be really difficult to give him enough attention for the next few days with the final practices before the competition and then the competition itself.'

Just then, the door swung open and Camilla marched in, carrying her costume. 'Has anyone seen any of the frost fairies? Ah, there you are,' she said, spotting them as they plumped up some cushions, twenty of them fluttering around one cushion and tossing it into the air before pulling it into place on the sofa.

They formed a cloud in the air, their faces enquiring and helpful. Camilla marched over to them.

'I want this changed!' She shoved her costume towards them. 'It's not right. It needs to be much tighter.'

The frost fairies spoke in their high-pitched voices. One of them pointed her

wand at a pile of paper on the table and
sparkly words appeared on it: *We'll alter it
as soon as we can*.

'See that you do,' Camilla said and she
turned and marched out.

Emily saw the frost fairies exchange
looks. From the way they rustled their
wings and put their hands on their hips,
she had a feeling they weren't very
impressed. But Camilla's demand had
given her an idea. She grabbed a piece
of paper and began to draw a skating
dress.

'What are you doing?' asked Tilda
curiously.

'I've had an idea,' Emily said. 'Hang on
a minute.' She coloured the dress sea
green, but made it look as if it was a
floaty fabric and added an underskirt of

deep blue. She drew in silver sequins around the waist and neckline.

'That looks like Hannah's dress, but much nicer,' said Tilda.

Emily nodded and labelled everything so that the drawing was clear. Then she approached the frost fairies, who had started tidying up the pens and pencils around the room.

'Um, hi,' Emily said politely. They stopped and flew up to look at her. Three of them perched on her shoulders. She smiled at them. 'Look, you can say no if it's too much work, but I was just wondering if you could possibly make another costume. I know it's short notice,' she said hurriedly. 'But it's not for me – it's for Hannah. She's a bit upset about the costume she has at

the moment. But if you can't, that's
fine —'

The frost fairies interrupted her,
speaking all at once. One took her
drawing, another fluttered up and gave
her a kiss on the cheek and then they all
nodded. The one who had taken the
drawing pointed her wand at the paper
on the table and a message appeared: *It'll*

*be ready on the day of the competition. We'd
be delighted to help!*

Emily smiled at them. 'Thanks!'

Alice squeezed her arm. 'That was a
really nice idea, Em.'

'I hope Hannah thinks so,' said Emily,
suddenly wondering if Hannah might be
offended.

'Well, she's always got the other dress if
she doesn't want to wear the new one,'
Tilda pointed out. 'And I'm sure she'll
think it's a lovely thought.'

Emily really hoped so!

## Chapter Eight
## Flying High

Emily spent as much of the next two days as she could with Molly. She even missed chances to do extra skating practice. But suddenly the competition didn't seem as important to her. *So what if I don't win?* she thought. *I'll do my best in it, but it's more important to be with Molly while she's injured.* Charlie was a good distraction, but Emily knew Molly really liked her visits too.

However, strangely, even though she wasn't practising as hard, Emily's skating started to improve again. On Saturday morning, before their skating lesson, she went through her routine. Starting in the centre of the ice and imagining the music in her head, Emily set off. Move began to follow move easily. While most of her mind was focused on the skating, Emily felt excitement growing. She felt

light and balanced and she was getting every move right. It was a very good feeling.

Tilda and Alice both clapped as she finished the final spin. Glowing with delight, Emily went over to the side to get her breath back.

Madame Letsworth was there. 'Well done, Emily. That's the best I've seen you skate in a few days.'

Emily smiled. Even though Madame Letsworth wasn't her official skating teacher, Emily had the feeling that nothing escaped the headteacher's eagle eyes. 'Thank you,' she said. 'I'm really surprised. I haven't practised much the last few days because I've been so busy with Molly. I thought I'd be awful!'

Madame Letsworth smiled back.

'Skating isn't just about practising. It *is* important, but to skate well you must also feel good about yourself inside.' Her eyes met Emily's. 'You may not have been practising much for the last few days, but you have been doing something much more important by helping a friend who is in need. You know you have been doing the right thing and that has helped your skating.' Her eyes twinkled. 'Of course, that doesn't mean you can stop practising altogether though, Emily!'

'I wouldn't ever do that. I love skating!' Emily declared.

'It's in your heart,' Madame Letsworth said softly. 'There's no doubt about that.'

Emily skated away. As she glided round the rink, she thought over what

Madame Letsworth had said about being happy and how that affected her skating. It was true, she realized. She'd felt different skating in the last few days since she had been helping Molly, lighter somehow and happier inside – much better than when she had been wrapped up in practising and thinking only about winning. *The pink skates are very important*, she thought, *but not as important as my friends.*

'So how was skating?' asked Molly when Emily went up to see her after the lesson.

'Really good!' Emily enthused.

'That's great!' said Molly. 'I can't believe it's the competition tomorrow. I wonder what Hannah will say when she sees her new dress.'

'I hope she likes it,' said Emily
anxiously.

'Oh, she'll love it!' Molly declared.
'You're such a good friend, Em, to think
of doing that.'

'I should have realized earlier that
Hannah needed help with it,' Emily
sighed. 'I've not been a good friend. I
should have done something about that,
and I should have said something to you
about not doing that jump.' She looked
guiltily at Molly.

Molly frowned. 'Don't be silly. Even if
you had said something, you know I
wouldn't have listened. Getting injured
was my own stupid fault. I'd have only
told you that you were interfering if
you'd said something.' She met Emily's
eyes. 'You're a brilliant friend, Emily.

And to prove it, I'm planning a surprise for you after the competition tomorrow.'

Emily frowned. 'What surprise?'

'Duh! If I told you, it wouldn't be a surprise, but me, Charlie and the frost fairies have been sorting it all out!'

'Oh, go on, tell me,' begged Emily, intrigued.

But no matter how much she pleaded, Molly refused to say any more. 'You'll find out tomorrow,' she kept repeating annoyingly. 'I'm not going to tell you now.'

Finally Emily gave up, but as she left Molly's room, she felt as if she was fizzing inside. What with the competition *and* a surprise, it looked like the next day was going to be very exciting indeed!

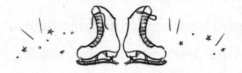

## Chapter Nine
### *The Competition*

The next morning, Emily was woken up by the sound of Hannah exclaiming, 'What's this?' She was staring at a parcel at the end of her bed.

Emily sat up. 'I hope you like it. I asked the frost fairies to make it for you. You don't have to wear it though,' she added hastily as Hannah started to unwrap the parcel. 'I just thought your dress could be a bit more exciting, but if you prefer to wear it . . .'

'No! This is gorgeous!' Hannah had taken the dress out and was holding it up. The frost fairies had done a fantastic job, making it just as Emily had designed.

'It'll look brilliant on you,' said Alice, getting out of bed.

'I can't wait to put it on!' Hannah ran over to Emily and hugged her. 'Thank

you so much, Em. You're amazing. When did you design it?'

'The other day.' Emily hugged her back. 'Do you really, really like it?' she said anxiously. 'You're not just saying that?'

Hannah's eyes shone. 'I love it!'

The morning flew by as the girls had a final practice session, got changed and then did their hair and make-up. Emily wore a sparkling blue eyeshadow that matched her dress, some blusher on her cheeks and a little lipstick. When they were all ready, she, Hannah, Alice and Tilda all went down to the common room.

'Oh, my goodness, look at Camilla!' whispered Emily.

Camilla was at the far side of the room in her silver catsuit. She was looking very pleased with herself as Tasha and the other Snow Foxes clustered round, oohing and ahhing. 'I know. It's cool, isn't it?' she said loudly.

'However is she going to skate in that?' Hannah muttered to Emily.

Emily could see what Hannah meant. The frost fairies had made the catsuit as tight as possible, just as Camilla had asked for. It didn't look very comfortable at all. Emily was very glad she was wearing her soft, sparkly, blue dress and Hannah looked beautiful in her sea-green costume. She had threaded silver and green ribbons into her hair and used a lot of eye make-up.

Hannah stroked the floaty skirt. 'I feel

so wonderful wearing this,' she said to Emily. 'I know it's going to make me skate my best!'

By eleven o'clock the girls were all ready and waiting in the changing area. The three skating teachers who were judging the competition were sitting at their table in the front row. The other seats were full of ice sylphs from the town who had arrived on big sleighs pulled by silver deer and huskies. The sound of the audience talking and the seats creaking made Emily's tummy feel funny. It was the first time she had skated in front of a big crowd.

Frost fairies were dancing around in the air above the judges' table. After each girl had skated and been given two marks by each of the three judges, one for technical ability and one for artistic interpretation, the fairies were going to fly up and form the total mark in the air.

At long last, Madame Letsworth skated on to the ice and a hush fell. 'Welcome to our Ice-skating Academy,' she declared in her musical voice. 'As you know, one of the girls you see skating here tonight will be chosen to be our Ice Princess in two weeks' time. The girls still know very little about what this will involve or, indeed, how we are going to choose the Ice Princess.'

She turned to look at the girls waiting in the changing area. 'You have been very patient and I promise that next week you will learn more about the task and about the qualities we are looking for in the Ice Princess.'

Emily exchanged excited looks with Hannah and Molly. She was longing to find out more about what the Ice Princess would actually have to do and how the teachers were going to choose her. Surely it was something to do with the competitions? But then again, maybe it wasn't.

Madame Letsworth turned back to the audience. 'Today all the girls have been asked to prepare a short routine with certain set elements. They have also chosen their own music and designed their own costumes. Please enjoy their performances!' She skated off to loud applause and took her place at the judges' table.

'I'm so nervous I can't breathe!' Emily said to Molly, who had begged to be allowed to sit with the other girls in the changing area. She had Charlie on her knee.

'You'll be fine,' she said to Emily. 'I know you will.'

'Better than fine,' Hannah chipped in. 'You'll be brilliant!'

Just then, Madame Longley opened the entrance barrier for Zoe, the first skater, to go on to the ice.

The competition had begun!

It was wonderful to watch everyone skate and hear the clapping at the end of each performance. It was just like Emily had imagined being a real ice-skater in the human world would be. She couldn't wait for her turn – she was skating fifth, after Heather.

*Oh, I hope I do well*, thought Emily as Heather got her marks – twenty-five, a low score, but she had kept her routine simple and easy.

Madame Longley, who was by the entrance, smiled at Emily. 'It's your turn now, Emily. On you go.'

Emily took a deep breath and skated on to the ice. She felt tense and horribly

nervous as everyone clapped her. She was
sure she was going to do something
wrong. Reaching the centre of the rink,
she took up her starting position – one
leg behind the other, hands and eyes
down.

The lights faded. Emily felt as if she
was about to explode with tension, but
then the music began! She pushed
forward and after the first few steps
everything faded away – the audience,
the thoughts of what jumps she was
going to do. She had been over the
routine so many times she barely had to
think what came next and instead felt as
if she was really becoming a bird,
swooping and diving. Each move flowed
effortlessly into the next with no
mistakes.

As the piece of music built to the finale, Emily reached the centre of the rink and started to spin. Round and round she went, arms above her head, until, with perfect timing, she stopped on the last beat. Throwing her arms out, she beamed in delight.

The audience clapped and cheered. Emily grinned, feeling as if there were fireworks going off inside her. She'd done it! She hadn't fallen or made any big mistakes.

She skated off the ice and the waiting girls surrounded her, calling out congratulations. All except Camilla. She stood aloof, her face calm and smugly composed. Hannah hugged Emily. 'You were great, Em! I bet you get a really good mark.'

The mark went up – thirty-one and a half out of thirty-six. Emily was in the lead! There was still a long way to go, she knew, and some really good routines to come, but she was very happy.

It was Hannah next. 'Good luck!' Emily called and, feeling very relieved that her turn was over, she went to sit with Molly.

The sequins on Hannah's costume sparkled in the spotlights. It looked lovely now, just right for her mermaid routine. The music started and she was off, dancing and spinning. She looked completely confident and relaxed as she performed all her really difficult jumps, a smile on her face as she landed each one. No one else had tried a routine that was anything like as hard as Hannah's and her final spin was so fast that she seemed to blur on the ice.

When she stopped, the crowd erupted. 'Oh wow, oh wow, oh wow!' gasped Molly, clapping as hard as she could. 'She's *got* to win with that!' She caught herself. 'Sorry, Em, I didn't mean to make it sound like I was saying your routine wasn't any good or anything.'

'It's OK. That was a brilliant routine,' said Emily. 'Hannah'll easily beat my marks – and she should.' She didn't feel unhappy though. She was proud of the mark she had got, but Hannah's routine had been better than hers and she wanted her friend to win. She deserved to.

Hannah skated off the ice. Emily hurried over to her just as the mark went up. 'Thirty-three!' she gasped. 'Oh,

Hannah! Well done!' Hannah squealed
and hugged her.

'No one's going to beat that,' declared
Molly in excitement.

'Oh, yeah?' Camilla's voice cut in.
'We'll see about that. Nice try, Hannah,
but prepare to come second.'

'Oh, just ignore her,' Emily said

quickly as Camilla tossed her hair back
and skated on to the ice.

'Don't worry, I will,' said Hannah.

'That catsuit is *very* tight!' commented
Molly.

Camilla started to skate. She landed her
double toe loop–double lutz
combination. Emily frowned. She could
almost see the shiny silver material
stretching at the seams as Camilla
gathered herself to launch into a double
axel. 'I hope it doesn't –' She broke off
with a gasp, a sound that was echoed by
the whole audience.

As Camilla had taken off into the air,
her costume had split slightly across her
bottom. She stumbled out of the jump,
her hands flying behind her to hold the
material together. It was so funny that

Emily couldn't help but giggle. She wasn't alone. The whole of the audience was laughing.

Camilla's face went bright red. She turned and skated off the ice as fast as she could. When she reached the barrier, she barged through the other girls, who were all looking torn between being shocked and amused, and went straight over to a cloud of frost fairies who were near the doors.

'This is all your fault!' Camilla screamed at them.

They held out their tiny hands and shook their heads as if they didn't know what she was talking about.

'Oh . . . GRRR!' she cried and stormed away.

## Chapter Ten

### *A Brilliant Surprise!*

The last few skaters performed their routines and the final marks were given out. Hannah had won! Emily had just been beaten by Amanda and so she came third. But she was very happy with that.

Hannah went to collect the pretty pink skates from Madame Letsworth. Molly and Emily both clapped and cheered along with everyone else as Hannah was presented with them and then Molly turned to Emily. 'I'm going to go and get your surprise ready. Come up to the dorm with Hannah in ten minutes. But not before – promise?'

'I promise,' said Emily. She was longing to find out what the surprise was!

By the time Hannah got off the ice and had spoken to all the people who wanted to congratulate her, the changing room had emptied and the other girls had disappeared. Emily waited for Hannah and they eventually headed back to the Frost Fairies dorm together.

'You were amazing,' Emily said.

Hannah smiled. 'Partly thanks to you. I love the dress and I just felt so happy wearing it, it made me feel like I could

do anything. I'm so glad Molly is
organizing this surprise for you.'

'Do you know what it is?' Emily asked
her.

Hannah grinned and nodded. 'Yep, but
I'm not saying cos Molly will kill me!'

As they reached the corridor, Emily
saw Alice looking out of the dorm. She
saw them, gave a squeak that made her

sound very like Charlie and shut the door quickly.

'What's up with Alice?' Emily said in astonishment. Hannah just grinned.

They reached the door and Emily opened it. The dorm was in darkness, the curtains shut. She started to frown. *What's going on . . . ?*

'SURPRISE!'

Molly, Tilda and Alice leapt out from their hiding places and Hannah turned the lights on. The dorm had been decorated with pink and lilac streamers. A table had been put in the room and covered with a silver tablecloth. On it were sandwiches and strawberries and a massive pink cake with a pair of white ice-skating boots made out of icing sugar on top. Frost fairies fluttered through the air, swooping and diving, their wings sparkling, and on Molly's bed bounced eight of the ice dragons who worked in the school.

Emily gaped. She didn't know what to say.

'Happy non-birthday!' cried Molly. The others echoed it and crowded round to hug Emily.

'Oh . . . wow!' Emily burst out.

'I know it's not your real birthday yet, but I thought you should have something. I'd have gone mad the last few days without you. You've been such a good friend,' Molly said.

'To me too,' said Hannah. 'It was so lovely of you to organize a new dress for me.'

'Charlie wants to say thank you too,' said Alice. 'He would have been very bored if you hadn't thought of a way to help him.'

There was a loud chirrup. Emily looked at the ice dragons and saw Charlie. He was still a lot smaller than the others, but he looked like he was having a great time with them, nuzzling and flapping his wings.

'He's been growing so fast he's big enough now to go and live with the other dragons properly,' said Tilda. 'Madame Longley said he can help in one of the music boxes.'

'So?' demanded Molly, looking at Emily eagerly. 'Are you pleased?'

Emily could hardly believe it all. 'Oh, yes!' she said, looking round at the decorated room, the party tea, the frost fairies and ice dragons . . .

Molly grinned. 'Then let's get partying!'

They ate and drank and chatted and then Emily blew out the candles on the cake. The news of the party had spread and other people kept joining them. Soon everyone was there – everyone apart from Camilla.

Emily looked round the room at the happy faces. It was wonderful having everyone there, but she didn't like the feeling that someone was missing. She hesitated and then turned to Hannah. 'I'll be back in a minute.'

She went down the stairs to the Snow Foxes dorm and knocked on the door. There was no answer. She pushed the door open, wondering what she would find. Maybe Camilla would be crying in there? As Emily peeped in, she saw Camilla, but she wasn't crying. She was lying on her bed, arms crossed, face sulky.

'What do you want?' she demanded.

'Come and join the party,' Emily said to her. Camilla looked surprised.

'Oh, come on,' Emily said quietly. 'Everyone's there. You should be too. I'd really like you to.'

Camilla hesitated and then huffed as if she was doing Emily a great big favour. 'Well, I *suppose* I could come.' She got up, grabbed a long cardigan from her wardrobe and joined Emily at the door. 'I'd have won, you know, if my costume hadn't split,' she muttered as she marched out.

Emily shook her head. Camilla could be really annoying, but even so, she was glad she was coming upstairs to join in. Emily knew she would enjoy the party much more if no one was left out.

When Emily got back, she found a pillow fight had broken out. The frost fairies were sitting up on the curtain rail and the ice dragons were watching from the windowsill. Everyone was laughing and screaming. As soon as Emily and Camilla walked through the door, they

got thumped with feather pillows.
Squealing, Emily grabbed a pillow from
the floor and joined in. Camilla only
hesitated a second before the sulky look
on her face faded and she joined in too,
hitting Tess and Olivia.

'Got you!' yelled Molly, thumping
Emily.

'Got you back!' Emily cried, swinging
the pillow towards her and then dodging
out of the way as Alice charged towards
her.

'Incoming . . . *wahhhh*!' Alice broke off
with a shriek as Tilda thwacked her legs
and she stumbled over.

The laughter and squealing rose and
the fight only ended when Molly hit
Hannah so hard the pillow burst and
clouds of white feathers flew into the air.

The girls all collapsed, giggling on the beds as the feathers floated down like snowflakes around them.

'Having a good time then?' said Molly to Emily as they lay on their backs on the bed.

'It's the best party I've ever had!' Emily declared. She sat up and looked round at everyone in the room. She'd only known them all for a few weeks, but it felt like forever. They were all so different from each other, but they were basically good friends and out of all of them only one was going to be chosen to be the Ice Princess.

*Who will it be?* thought Emily, looking round.

Her heart did a double flip. She couldn't wait to find out!

**Do you dream of becoming an Ice Princess?**

**Have you ever wanted to go to a REAL Skating School?**

**All readers of *Skating School* get FREE membership to the National Ice Skating Association's Skate UK programme!**

Skate UK will help you to learn all the moves and basic skills
you need to become a true Ice Princess! It's all about fun
and continuous movement and is taught in groups,
so why not share your love of *Skating School* with
your friends and bring them too?

To get your free membership, go to
**www.iceskating.org.uk/skatingschool**
and enter the secret password: **Twirl**.

Skate UK is taught by licensed NISA coaches and can be
assisted by trained Programme Assistants.

For full terms and conditions visit:
**www.lindachapman.co.uk**
**www.iceskating.org.uk/skatingschool**

**Do you want to enter super competitions, get sneak previews and download lots of** *Skating School* **fun?**

Get YOUR skates on
join the
**Sparkle Club**
today!

lindachapman.co.uk

Just enter this secret password:

## Twirl

The Land of Ice and Winter is waiting for you …

# Design your own ice-skating dress!

The tiny frost fairies have been working overtime designing the beautiful dresses for the girls to wear in the Ice-skating Academy competitions.

Using this dress as a template, the fairies need you to draw the most magical ice-skating outfit you can think of. Every month one lucky winner will receive a magical *Skating School* goody bag!

Send your drawing
with your name and address to:

Skating School Competition, Puffin Marketing, 80 Strand, London WC2R 0RL

Or e-mail them to: **skatingschool@uk.penguingroup.com**

# Welcome back to the magical Land of Ice and Winter

## … a world where all your dreams come true!

A brand-new

*Skating School* series

Coming soon!

Hi there,

I hope you've enjoyed reading about the adventures of the girls who go to the Magic Ice-skating Academy. I love writing them all down! Wouldn't it be amazing to go to the Land of Ice and Winter and see all the creatures who live there? Can you imagine holding an actual ice dragon or talking to a frost fairy?

Sometimes readers write to me and ask about my life. Being a writer is the best job ever. I live in a cottage in a village with my family and two dogs – a Bernese mountain dog and a golden retriever. I spend my days writing and going to visit schools and libraries to talk about writing.

I always think I'm really lucky because I get to spend my days writing about magic – mermaids, unicorns, stardust spirits, genies and now the Land of Ice and Winter. If you love them too then why not go to **www.lindachapman.co.uk** and join the Sparkle Club? It's my online fan club with loads of activities and downloads, and you can only get to it by using the secret password at the back of this book. Have fun!

Love,

*Linda*
xxx